THE RESCUE

And Other Tales

This collection copyright 2017

©Steven A. McKay

Contents

Foreword

Welcome to this collection of Forest Lord short tales! Pour yourself a drink, grab some snacks and put your feet up before we head once more into the greenwood with Robin and friends.

This little book gathers together three stories which have never been published in paperback form before: "The Escape", "The Rescue", and *The Prisoner* (which is a novelette so gets italics instead of inverted commas in case you thought that was a formatting error). They all slot into the full Forest Lord timeline which I will list at the back of book if you want to read the stories in the order they were intended. All three work fine on their own though, so if you want to just dive in and start reading that's okay.

I had a *lot* of fun writing these three tales and I hope that comes across as you read them. A short story or novelette has obvious limitations in terms of character development and complexity of plots but they also allow a writer to just get right down to business and I believe that makes this a nice addition to the novels and novellas already published.

If you like audiobooks Nick Ellsworth has already started recording this collection for Audible so look out for it.

On with the action.

Enjoy!

THE
ESCAPE

BARNSLEY, NORTHERN ENGLAND

APRIL 1323 A.D.

"More ale!"

That had been the war-cry of John Little and his two companions for most of the afternoon and, now, when the sun was at last beginning to set, the giant outlaw's thirst seemed as great as ever.

The harassed landlord eventually hurried over to their table, placing another three brimming mugs down and lifting the empties, smiling in thanks as John handed him coin enough for the drinks and a small tip.

It was Wednesday, and that meant market day in Barnsley. John, a bear of man standing almost seven feet tall with a wild brown beard, had come to the Yorkshire town that morning with his friend Robin Hood to see what the merchants had to offer and to enjoy the locals' hospitality.

Ever since Robin had defeated King Edward II's bounty hunter, Sir Guy of Gisbourne – taking the man's eye and almost his life in the process – things had been quiet for their gang. The law had, for a few months at least, stopped hunting them so relentlessly and, as a result, they'd taken the opportunity to visit families and friends in their villages all over Yorkshire.

There were rumours that Sir Guy, nicknamed The Raven by superstitious folk, was on the mend and might be on the lookout for the outlaws again but, so far, they were unconfirmed and so Robin and John weren't too worried about being captured.

Today the two friends had looked at the wares displayed on Barnsley's gaudy stalls, sampled the meat pies and other hot savouries on offer and Robin had bought a simple but pretty necklace for his wife, Matilda, along with a little set of wooden animals for his infant son.

John, famously known as *Little* John, also bought a nice piece of jewellery for his wife, Amber. His own son was, at ten summers, much too old for toys; instead, the big wolf's head had paid for a fine hunting bow which was bigger and more powerful than the one the lad had been practising with for a couple of years.

After they'd been around all the stalls, which didn't take that long, they made their way to the nearest inn for some refreshment.

Robin only stayed for a short time before saying his goodbyes to John and the two townsfolk, Edwin and Algar – previous acquaintances – who'd joined their company after the market. His wife frightened Robin much more than the sheriff's foresters did, so, despite John loudly calling his manhood into question, the young outlaw captain had gone home in good spirits, exhorting the giant not to get into any trouble. He'd taken the bow for John's son with him, to save his friend carrying it around all night and possibly misplacing it.

"This is the busiest I can remember Barnsley," Little John said to the two locals as they hoisted their freshly filled mugs aloft and looked around at the bustling alehouse, his eyes settling on a group of rowdy drinkers at a table nearby. "Some of these lads don't look like they're here just to stock up on fish and rolls of cloth either."

Edwin took a sip and nodded agreement. "You're right. That lot are Scots; mercenaries. Listen to them, I can't understand a damn word they're saying."

"They're on their way to Sussex," Algar stated, matter-of-factly, as if he knew all about the dangerous-looking men drinking and joking noisily in the corner of the large common room. "Some lord down there has connections with Scotland and sent for men to help him fight off marauding outlaws or the like." He shrugged, his knowledge exhausted, but a small, satisfied smile played around his lips as he helped himself to another swig of ale.

Algar liked nothing better than knowing what was going on in Barnsley and he'd listened surreptitiously earlier in the afternoon, as the landlord had told another patron all about the Scottish mercenaries.

"Well, good luck to them," Edwin shrugged. "As long as they keep themselves to themselves. Bastards did a lot of damage when they were raiding our towns and villages not so long ago."

Little John nodded. The Scots had indeed caused a lot of trouble for the people of Yorkshire in recent years but King Edward II, or his advisers at least, seemed to have negotiated an uneasy peace with the Scottish ruler, Robert the Bruce. For now at least. As a result, Yorkshire and its environs had of late been spared the bloody raids from the madmen in the dark northern reaches of the island.

"More –"

"Ale?" The serving girl broke in just as the big outlaw raised his arm to hail the landlord on the far side of the room. She leaned down to look at him, her loose tunic giving John a tantalising view of the swell of her breasts, and grinned. Everyone in Barnsley knew the friendly giant with his easy smile and enormous quarterstaff which he carried everywhere.

"No!" John shook his head, laughing at the young girl's look of surprise. "Food. More of that pottage we had earlier, please, lass. I'm bloody starving."

"Aye," Algar grinned. "Me too."

"And," Edmond put in as the girl turned to make her way to the kitchen. "More ale!"

* * *

"What's that big bastard staring at?" the Scotsman growled as he noticed the hirsute local looking in their direction. "I'll take that crazy beard aff his face with my dagger if he keeps lookin' over here."

The other mercenaries knew better than to turn and look at the man their mate was glaring at. Knew better than to attract attention to themselves. Starting a fight in a tavern full of Englishmen didn't seem like a sensible idea at all.

"Keep your voice down, Angus," muttered one of them, the oldest in their party with close-cropped grey hair and a neat beard to match, laying a firm restraining hand on the younger man's arm. "Look at the size of him for God's sake, he's a giant. Am not wantin' to start any shit with a man as big as that."

Angus pulled his arm away with a grimace. "That's because yer a craven, Balfour. The bigger they are, the harder they fall. Am no' afraid of the giant. He's no' that much bigger than me anyway."

"Enough." Another of the Scots broke in softly, fixing the irritable Angus with a steely glare. "Ye'll no' be starting any trouble here. Now hold yer peace before the whole town gives us a good kickin'."

The voice was calm but it was full of quiet power despite the speaker's diminutive stature, and Angus fell silent with a sheepish glance at the man who was obviously the mercenaries' leader.

"All right, Duncan, I was just sayin'."

"Ye said enough, boy. Now shut yer piehole."

Duncan was the smallest man in the Scottish party but he had a disconcerting stare that could reduce most men to silence. Thirty-two years old, with dark, almost black, hair, it seemed his ancestry was part Gaelic, part Mediterranean. He wore brown hose and leather boots, while a faded grey tunic covered his gambeson. At his side he wore a short sword rather than the great claymores of his companions. The tip of such a massive blade might well have trailed along the ground if Duncan had tried wearing one on his belt.

Yet, although the rest of the Scottish mercenaries – seven of them – were taller, broader, drunker and carried much more imposing weaponry about them, not one of them was as menacing as Duncan.

When he spoke, his companions shut their mouths and listened.

"Look at the way the people watch him," the Scot said, gesturing discreetly towards Little John. "Everyone seems to know him and everyone either fears or respects him."

His companions said nothing, wondering where he was going with this line of thought.

"Yet... see the way he carries himself? Look at him now, sittin' there, hunched inside his cloak." Duncan raised a quizzical eyebrow, his soft voice somehow carrying to all his companions despite the rowdy atmosphere inside the tavern. "It's as if he doesnae want to attract attention to himself, even though the fawning locals either want to buy him a drink or have his baby, and when he stands up he almost hits his head aff the damn roof."

"Go on," Balfour nodded. "Whit're ye gettin' at, lad?"

Duncan shook his head, eyes wide in theatrical disbelief.

"Av surrounded maself wi a buncha idiots. Is it no obvious?" He gazed over at the bearded, enormous Yorkshireman who sat, smiling innocently, almost childlike, as one of his mates told a story.

"The giant is a wolf's head."

"A what?" Angus wondered, tipping the last of his ale into his mouth and belching loudly.

"An outlaw! What are we here for?" Duncan demanded, catching Angus and the other men off guard with the change in the conversation. "Why are we on our way to Sussex at all?"

"Money," Balfour replied, while the other men chimed in with, "gold!", "coin!" or "silver!"

"Exactly," the little Scot nodded, staring across the tavern at Little John, a lupine smile on his face. "Well, I can guarantee there will be a huge blood-price on that giant's head, and we can collect it tonight. Dead or alive. And I'll wager *dead* will be much easier than trying to capture the big bastard in one piece..."

* * *

"I think I've had enough for one night, lads." Little John smiled, sinking the last of the dregs in his mug and placing a small coin on the table for the serving girl when she came to clear away their empties.

Algar sat back on his stool with a look of disgust. "Ah, big man, you're not the drinker you used to be. Leaving so early? When you can still walk straight?"

John laughed at the jibe although, in truth, he'd very rarely been so drunk he couldn't walk properly. He had a huge capacity for drink and, like his young captain Robin, didn't enjoy the loss of self-control that extreme inebriation brought. "Aye, I can still walk," he grinned. "And give you a slap too, if there's any more of your shit, Algar."

Edwin drained his own ale and nodded, placing a hand on the table to steady himself as he got to his feet. "Aye, fair enough, John. Come on Algar, up. I've got to get to my workshop in the morning anyway. If I drink much more ale I'll be late starting *and* spew my guts up all day. Let's go. You can stay the night at my place; it'll be cheaper than paying for a room here."

John smiled and slapped the man on the back, although he made sure he did it gently. The combination of his prodigious strength and Edwin's drunken state might otherwise have resulted in the man flying halfway across the inn to land in an embarrassing heap at the feet of the Scottish mercenaries that had been throwing the outlaw curious, and none-too-friendly, glances all night.

As the three companions waved and shouted their goodbyes to the landlord and serving girls, John looked down at the Scots but not one of them met his eye and the giant knew instinctively that something was amiss.

They stumbled out into the cool night air which felt good on their skin after the stuffy atmosphere inside the tavern.

"Come on, which way to your house?" John asked Edwin, wanting to be away and off the streets as soon as possible. Strangely, he was completely at home in the pitch black greenwood with Robin Hood and the lads but... being in a town at night made him nervous and watchful. Most men would surely have felt exactly the opposite, but John had never liked enclosed spaces.

"Along this way," Edwin replied. "Algar's house is on the same street as mine, just a few doors away. C'mon... follow me."

The trio began to walk along the road, dimly lit by the gibbous moon in the cloudy sky and the occasional torch that burned along the way to guide locals to their homes in the dark.

"Hurry up," John growled as Algar stopped, facing the wall of a house and fiddling with his breeches.

"Need a piss," the man slurred, the sound of splattering confirming his assertion.

"Aye, so do I now you mention it," Edwin decided, undoing the laces on his own hose and, drawing himself to full-height he arched his back and stared directly up at the stars overhead as he relieved himself right in the middle of the road.

John sighed and waited impatiently.

Finally, with satisfied grunts, the men adjusted their breeches and the small party walked on again, Algar and Edwin's voices jarringly loud as they chattered inanely in the darkness.

"Wait!" John, who walked ahead of the other two, raised a massive arm, halting the progress of his companions. He turned, finger raised to his lips and looked back along the street, eyes narrowed in concentration.

The sound of the tavern door opening and closing carried to them and Algar irritably screwed up his eyes. "What –"

The murderous glare John threw him shut his mouth with an almost audible snap and the three men stood in silence again, listening.

By now, Algar and Edwin knew something wasn't quite right. John was used to living in the forest on the edge of his wits, senses attuned to any sign of approaching danger. The giant's behaviour was beginning to frighten them.

For his part, John knew the Scots in the tavern had been watching him for a reason. He wondered if they'd been sent by the sheriff, Sir Henry de Faucumberg, or even the king, to round up the few remaining rebels from the failed Lancastrian revolt. Or maybe they were Sir Guy of Gisbourne's men? If they were they'd know exactly who John was – no one else in Yorkshire stood as tall as he did.

Whoever they were, those Scots were trouble, John knew that much.

"You two get off home now, move it."

"What about you?" Edwin wondered. "Where are you going to sleep off that ale?"

The street behind them was unnaturally silent which only made John even more certain that the mercenaries were coming for him and, possibly, his two innocent companions as well.

"Don't worry about me," he growled, shoving the two men in the back and waving them away. "Just get yourselves home and bar the doors behind you." He hefted his absolutely enormous quarterstaff which was just as tall as he was and grinned. "I have some business to take care of."

* * *

"I cannae hear them. Are you sure they came along this way?"

"Shut the hell up," Duncan hissed, glaring murderously at the man who'd spoken. "They came this way. I was watching them from behind the door." He pointed as they walked silently along the street, the two still gently steaming wet patches on the ground confirming his statement. "Now keep yer mouths shut and listen out for them."

The Scots padded along making barely a sound although they'd all drank at least as much ale as Edwin and Algar. Their hands were on the hilts of their swords but the blades remained safely hidden inside their scabbards – if some local opened his door unexpectedly the sight of eight armed Scotsmen wandering along the road would surely have brought a storm of unwanted attention down upon them.

It made things easier for Little John though.

His two friends were long gone, disappeared safely into the darkness now that they – vaguely – understood that they were in some kind of danger. The huge wolf's head stood in a gloomy alley just off the main street, pressed against the wall of a house, as the mercenaries approached making barely a sound.

John waited, allowing the men to pass. When the last of them was abreast of him he raised his staff and rammed the point into the Scotsman's temple sending the man reeling face-first into the street; comatose or dead, the giant didn't know or care.

The sound of their companion's fall brought the rest of the Scots up short, every one of them trying to haul their swords free as fast as possible but John was still in motion, his staff, as thick as a man's wrist, snaking out to crack the skull of another of the mercenaries, then, reversing the weapon's momentum, he brought it around and into the ankles of another target. The man dropped to the ground with a desperate cry before John silenced him with a brutal kick in the mouth.

In a matter of moments the big outlaw had taken three of his stalkers out of the fight and confusion reigned in the moonlit street. John knew better than to try and fight eight men at once though, and he slipped back into the shadows as the Scots hissed at one another demanding to know what in the name of God had just happened to their mates.

John ran quietly down the alley, hoping he'd done enough to stop his pursuers. He cursed though, as the sound of the remaining Scots' footsteps came to him, charging along behind him, furious oaths on their lips.

He reached the end of the alleyway but it was almost pitch black and he didn't know Barnsley very well at all. He had no idea where to run. The street led onto a wide, seemingly main thoroughfare, which ran off to either side but, for all John knew one or the other way led to a dead end and five against one wasn't odds even the big outlaw fancied.

Once again he pressed himself against the wall of the corner house, hugging the shadows which concealed his enormous bulk, and waited for his pursuers, blood thundering in his veins at the night's unexpected excitement.

The Scots made far too much noise as they came after him and, as the first of them reached the end of alleyway, John swung his quarterstaff in a vicious arc right into the man's face. With a horrific, sickening crack the pursuer was thrown backwards, his face a

11

ruined, bloody mess.

John transferred the staff to his left hand and, with his right, drew his dagger from his belt as the next Scot charged at him, sword drawn. The bearded outlaw feinted to the side then, as his assailant stumbled to meet him, John rammed the point of his knife deep into the man's windpipe.

Leaving his dagger in the dying man's neck the wolf's head ran off again into the moonlit shadows.

"He went that way!"

The pounding footsteps barely slowed as the remaining three Scotsmen charged after him. John tried to increase his pace but the large amount of ale and stew he'd consumed that night combined to make his legs leaden and he knew he wouldn't be able to run for much longer. He had a feeling the last of his pursuers would prove to be the smartest of them too; and by far the most dangerous.

His heart sank even further when he turned a corner and heard one of the mercenaries whoop in delight from behind.

"He's run into a dead end! The big bastard's ours now."

* * *

John set his feet defensively, hefting his great quarterstaff as the smallest of the Scotsmen, obviously their leader, walked into the street with a look of pure rage on his face. He led his final two companions, Angus and Balfour – who was blowing hard – in a loose triangular formation with himself at the front.

"You great turd, you've taken out half of my men.

That's going to cost me a lot of money since the lordling that hired me wanted eight soldiers, not three!" The wiry little man pointed the tip of his sword towards John. "You might be double my size but I'm going to use this to cut off your balls and eat them."

John raised an eyebrow at the bizarre threat. "You'd like having my balls in your mouth, wouldn't you? But it's not going to happen, you little rat-bastard. Come on, what are you waiting for? I've already taken down five of you northern maids, let's end this now so I can be on my way."

Angus was enraged, both at the loss of his companions and the confident smile of the huge bearded outlaw. Balfour, on the other hand, older and more experienced, watched their target uneasily, wondering if they'd bitten off more than they could chew. The wolf's head had killed or otherwise incapacitated five – five! – hard men as if it was nothing.

"On my command," Duncan growled softly, eyes boring into Little John murderously, "rush him with me, Balfour. Angus, you dodge around behind him and see if you can skewer the big prick while he's trying to hold us off."

"That won't work," John laughed, overhearing the man's plan. "I'll –"

"Now!"

Duncan ran forward swinging his sword inwards to try and take John in the midriff while Balfour followed a moment later, bringing his sword up overhead, ready to bring it down in a brutal killing blow. Angus scurried to the side, keeping as much space between himself and the outlaw as possible to

13

avoid the reach of the long staff that had brutalized so many of his mates already that night.

John gripped his weapon in both hands, swaying to the right to deflect Duncan's blade. The dark Scot stumbled under the force of the parry while the outlaw, without pausing, twirled the staff in a surprisingly agile move that caught Balfour's sword on the downstroke, halting its momentum. Little John then leaned in close to the older Scot and brought his knee up, hammering it between the man's legs with eye-watering force.

Angus managed to get around behind the giant but he didn't attack just yet, wary of the enormous quarterstaff still held firmly in John's hands.

"You could eat your mate's bollocks instead of mine," the big outlaw grunted at Duncan, nodding down at the fallen, mewling Balfour who lay in the street curled up like a fifty-year-old foetus. "Although I think I probably just burst them." He swung his staff around, pushing back the last of the Scotsmen, wondering how he could possibly fend off an attack from both front and back.

The street *was* a dead-end though...

With the loudest roar either of his assailants had ever heard come out of a human mouth, Little John turned and charged at the wide-eyed, stunned Angus.

The Scot stumbled backwards, sword held up defensively. He liked to think he was a cold-blooded killer; a mercenary that any nobleman would want to hire. But the sight and sound of the murderous giant coming towards him assailed his senses and, when he felt his back come up, hard, against the stone wall of a house, he panicked.

"No, leave me alone!"

The Scot tried feebly to ram his blade into John's guts but the heavy staff knocked it aside and John simply ran straight into the man, elbow first, crushing his head into the wall.

"Now." The outlaw spun round, ready to face the last of his attackers – their leader – supremely confident after defeating seven men without taking even a scratch himself.

But Duncan was faster and more skilled than his comrades.

As John turned, a savage blow battered him in the side and he roared in pain. His gambeson absorbed some of the force but the strike still hurt immensely. Even the smallest of men could learn how to land a blow with a force that belied their stature – apparently the dark-haired Scot had learned his violent trade well.

With a despairing gasp, John threw up the tip of his quarterstaff, into his attacker's blade, sending it spinning into the night and using his left hand to grab Duncan's tunic. They both fell, hard, onto the road with the Scot on top.

John still struggled for breath, but Duncan was fuelled by an insane rage and the mercenary used his bare hands to rain punches into the outlaw's face, grunting with every blow, teeth bared in a bitter smile as he sensed victory.

The outlaw did what he could to defend himself but the little man's blows were well-placed and he felt himself slipping into unconsciousness as punch after punch slammed into him.

Surprisingly, John didn't fear his inevitable death. The pain from his beating was already beginning to fade away and he could feel a warm glow spread through him, happy in the knowledge that he'd managed to beat seven men single-handedly. Seven! Wait until he told Robin and the rest of the lads this story...

Just before he blacked out another voice reached him. A familiar voice, although, at that moment John couldn't think where he'd heard it before.

Suddenly, the beating stopped and he felt the weight of his would-be killer lifted off his chest.

"Catch that grey-haired bastard," the new voice shouted. A confident voice, well-used to giving orders – a lawman. "He ran into that side street there. I want him caught."

Little John opened his eyes a crack and peered up groggily at his saviour. He was about to mumble his thanks but then he caught sight of the armour the man wore.

Groaning softly, he pulled his knees up into his chest to make himself look as small as possible, and hid his face in the cold earth of the road – and there he'd been thinking the night couldn't get much worse!

"Too many of them for the jail," the lawman spat. "Tie them up and put them in the barn next to it for the night. I'll question the scum in the morning."

He looked down at John.

"You all right, man? Your friends came and told us this lot were trying to rob you. You were lucky – bunch of amateurs obviously, or you'd not have escaped with your life."

"Thank you, my lord," John muttered. "You saved me."

"Need help to get home? No? Good. Be on your way then."

The lawman walked off, barking orders at his men

who were rounding up the surviving Scots.

John could hear Duncan's voice, raised in fury at being arrested, but the sound was abruptly cut off by a thump. One of the lawmen had apparently grown weary of the captive's objections and decided to silence it with more violence.

Good.

Little John desperately hauled himself to his feet with his staff and, holding onto the wall to steady himself, made his way out of the alley, stumbling as fast as he could in the opposite direction from the lawmen. He'd keep walking until he could get his bearings and then find a way into the trees that lay north of the small town.

What a night! He felt his body for broken bones, wincing as he touched his side. A couple of ribs cracked there by the little Scot's blade, he thought, but it could have been much worse if his gambeson hadn't turned the blow. Must have hit him with the flat rather than the full edge, thanks be to God.

Once he made it back to camp this would make a fine tale. Chased by a band of mad Scottish mercenaries, killing seven of them then, just as he was about to be beaten to death himself... along came his saviour.

Aye, Robin and the lads would love to hear how Little John's life had been saved by the very man tasked to hunt them down and bring them to justice by the king himself: Sir Guy of Gisbourne.

The Raven was back!

THE END

Author's Note

One thing that I've never really explored in my Forest Lord books is the idea that the villagers around Yorkshire might rebel against Robin Hood and his friends and turn them in to the law. Of course, our favourite outlaws are good to the locals – giving them food, money and protection against (other!) criminals – while making it clear anyone betraying them to the law can expect an unpleasant death.

But what if some *outsiders* were to show up? Hard men, with no loyalty to Robin's gang or any fear of their retribution?

It seemed an interesting idea and, being a Scot myself, I knew where those outsiders should come from. I would point out, though, that Little John is a giant and this is a work of fiction – eight Scotsmen would, easily, be able to hold their own against one Englishman in real-life. Aye, even a giant. We're a hardy race!

The Escape was conceived as a fun short story and I really hope you enjoyed it.

Steven A. McKay,
Old Kilpatrick,
February 2nd, 2017

THE
PRISONER

Northern England, 1325 AD

Winter

It was snowing hard, the wind whipping around the legs of their horses and inside the damp folds of their travel cloaks. Robert Hood, more commonly known as Robin, muttered an oath, was wishing he and his giant companion John Little – himself better known as Little John – were in a tavern somewhere closer to home.

The thought of a cosy, crackling log fire and a mug of warmed ale momentarily cheered him, until the gloom overwhelmed him once again and he remembered they were still at least an hour away from their destination.

"What do you think the sheriff will do with the rapist when we take him to Nottingham?" John shouted, his voice powerful enough to carry over the sound of hooves thudding into snow, and the gale that whistled through the bare trees flanking the road.

Robin shook his head and shouted in reply. "Probably abjuration. That's what usually happens to men like that."

"Serve the bastard right too," his giant lieutenant growled. "He deserves to be banished abroad. There's never any excuse for forcing a woman into your bed."

Both men had known rapists before in their experience, both as lawmen and when they'd been notorious, fabled outlaws themselves. They'd robbed and even killed people but never had they abused a woman in such a way, and they'd not allowed any of their old gang members to behave like that either.

Robin's thoughts inevitably turned to his wife, Matilda, at home in Wakefield with their son, Arthur, and from the pensive look on John's bearded face he guessed his giant friend was thinking along similar lines.

"Don't worry, John, this won't take us too long. We'll spend the night at Stapleford's inn – with a few ales and some stew to keep us company – then see the prisoner safely back to Nottingham. Unless Sir Henry has another job lined up for us, we'll be able to head home for a while. The sheriff's covering our expenses too, so eat as much of the food at the inn as you can stomach."

They shared a grin despite the weather and distance from their loved ones, pulling their cloaks tighter to try and stave off the worst of the biting chill.

"Aye, you're right," Little John agreed as their mounts picked their way along the treacherous road. "This should be an easy enough job."

* * *

When they reached Stapleford it was late in the day and there seemed little point in declaring themselves to the headman and locating the prisoner. What would be the point? They couldn't take the rapist back to Nottingham until morning anyway.

Instead, they stopped for a time to gaze up at a huge stone monolith that stood near the road, infinitely strange and mysterious in the surrounding flat landscape.

"Must be the Hemlock Stone," John guessed. "I've heard of it in passing. Apparently the devil threw it there because the sound of church bells pissed him off."

Robin looked at the sandstone monument which was three times as big as Little John and shook his head in wonder. "Maybe. I wouldn't believe every fanciful story you're told though."

The wind began to blow even harder, sending flurries of snow all around, so they moved on again, heading for the brightest-lit dwelling they could see as they rode into the main street – the alehouse.

The welcoming light, and smell, of a log fire filtered out from the two-storey building and they were drawn inexorably towards it, like moths to an open candle.

They found the cramped stable building that was attached to the inn and tethered their horses – all three of them, since they'd brought a spare to carry the prisoner – before hurrying inside and hailing the landlord.

"Well met, friend," Robin smiled. "We'll need a room for the night and some food and ale, if that's all right?"

"Aye, my lords," the man grinned, eyeing their weapons and good-quality, if simple, clothing. "We don't get many visitors during the winter months, for obvious reasons, so you're very welcome here. I'll see about your food right away. You take a seat there and warm yourselves." He gestured at a table by the crackling fire and turned away.

"Send your stable boy to see to our mounts, too, if you would," Robin shouted and was rewarded with a small wave of agreement and a shouted promise of oats and hay.

They seated themselves by the fire with sighs and broad smiles of satisfaction, rubbing their hands to bring some warmth back into them, basking in the glorious warmth which had already begun to thaw their icy fingers and toes and turn their cheeks red.

Soon enough the inn-keeper brought them two mugs of ale, gesturing to the pokers by the hearth which they might use to warm the drinks if they wished. When he wandered back to the kitchen Robin and John gladly placed the implements into the flames for a time then dipped them in the ale mugs, watching the dark liquid hiss as it heated invitingly. Soon, as they sat supping the wonderful, slightly herby drinks the man returned with two steaming bowls and a trencher laden with a loaf of black bread.

"Enjoy, my lads," he smiled, and his expression was one of a man who knew his food was sure to please. "If you want any more – and you will – just shout."

They set to with relish and soon finished the meal but, before they could even wave him over, the inn-keep had bustled across and set down second helpings, clearing their empty bowls away with a knowing, satisfied smile.

"Oh, this is the life," John gasped, as he swallowed another long pull of ale, and Robin nodded, mumbling an incoherent reply through a mouthful of the excellent stew.

As they devoured their second serving the alehouse door opened again and a flurry of snow whipped inside before the newcomer thrust it to and stamped his feet on the hard ground to remove the slush packed hard around them.

He was a slim fellow, of average height, with hard, confident eyes that swept the room before settling at last on Robin and John.

Robin watched the man as he strode across the small common room towards them, a smile appearing on his face as he neared their table.

"You must be the lawmen from Nottingham."

"Well spotted. What gave us away?"

The man pulled up a stool and sat next to them, not noticing or perhaps simply ignoring the gentle sarcasm in John's voice.

"We don't get many visitors around here, and even less as big as you two. Word came to me that you'd arrived, so here I am to greet you." He raised a hand to catch the burly inn-keeper's attention. "I'll be paying for the lads' meal and board, Simon. All right?"

The landlord nodded, gave a small grunt that might have meant anything, and went back to polishing the top of his bar with a filthy old rag that could only be spreading the grime about.

"There's no need for that, friend," Robin shook his head, assuming, correctly, that this newcomer must be the village headman. "The sheriff, Sir Henry, is covering all our expenses."

The man winked. "Sir Henry de Faucumberg is a cousin of mine, but he doesn't have to know that someone else paid for your stay here, does he? You two hold onto the coins he gave you. Go on, put them back in your purses. We'll see you right in Stapleford since you're here to do me – us – a good turn by taking that foul raper away."

He got to his feet and surprised, Robin swallowed a piece of breadas the man made to head back into the night.

"Won't you stop and have a drink with us?" the lawman shouted.

"No thank you, although God bless you for the thought. I've got work of my own to do this night and it can't wait. Head to the mill tomorrow – Simon will direct you although it's easy enough to find. The prisoner – Luke Tanner – is being held in the basement there for now, and I expect you'll want to get him back to the city as soon as possible, eh? See justice done?"

He waved merrily and, before the lawmen could utter another word, the door was opened with a chill blast and he was gone.

"Strange fellow," Robin muttered, thoughtfully tipping another spoonful of stew into his mouth. "I don't think I've ever met anyone like him before."

John simply shrugged, sighing as a sip of ale warmed his body. "Lots of people are strange. Let's just do as he says and enjoy the hospitality he's paying for. We can find out more about this whole business tomorrow, if you want."

"Aye, fair enough," Robin nodded drowsily. "I suppose you're right."

He finished his meal and leaning back in the creaking chair, patted his stomach, although the feeling of contentment was somewhat offset by the look he'd noticed on the inn-keeper's face when the headman was leaving.

Hate might have been too strong a word to describe the expression, but it was clear the jovial landlord had little time for the suave fellow.

"More ale," John called and, by now utterly relaxed, pulled off his damp boots and set stockinged feet towards the fire.

"No more food though," Robin joked, eyeing the giant's waggling, sweating toes theatrically. "I've just lost my appetite."

* * *

Through long habit both lawmen woke early the next morning despite the lack of any sunlight to suggest a new day was upon them. They dressed, checked their weapons were all strapped securely in place, and ate a frugal breakfast of bread and cheese which the bright-eyed inn-keeper insisted they have before they left.

The man escorted them to the door and pointed along the frosty street towards a structure which, despite the gloom, could be seen quite clearly thanks to its great bulk.

"There's the mill," he said, handing them full ale-skins and a pack stuffed with food. "Since William Broadhurst is paying for this I thought I might as well make sure you wouldn't go hungry or thirsty."

"William Broadhurst? That's the headman who came last night to see us?"

"Aye," the inn-keep nodded, a sneer creasing his upper lip momentarily, and Robin guessed the man must be jealous of Broadhurst who was handsome, confident and, judging by his dress and be-ringed fingers, extremely wealthy.

They thanked the landlord for his hospitality and headed towards the mill on foot.

The previous day's snow had left a crisp, fresh white carpet underfoot which crunched satisfyingly as they walked and it didn't take them very long to reach the squat building. The water wheel was turning at a steady, creaking pace and the presence of candle-light inside the mill suggested the miller was at work already, grinding grains into flour which he'd then sell on to the baker.

Robin rapped authoritatively on the wooden door and let himself in, followed by John.

"You'll be here for the prisoner?" shouted the miller, a short, well-muscled young man in his mid-twenties, over the noise of the grinding stones, without stopping his work or offering any other greeting. "He's down there." He nodded towards a trapdoor in the floor which was covered with heavy sacks of grain. "You'll need to shift those bags yourselves lads, shouldn't be too hard for men of your size." He smiled sheepishly. "Sorry there's so many of them piled up. Broadhurst didn't want any chance of the bastard escaping."

Rolling his eyes, Little John strode across and started tossing the sacks to the side effortlessly. Robin joined him and when they'd cleared the obstruction, pulled the trapdoor open revealing an inky blackness below.

The bailiff peered down into the chamber beneath, but it was impossible to see anything, so complete was the darkness.

"Luke Tanner? You down there? Come up," he shouted. "Now."

Robin was, by now, used to giving commands and his powerful voice seemed to persuade the captive below to come up without a fight as the rickety steps leading up towards them shook. A moment later a handsome man stepped into the room beside them. He appeared well-groomed despite his incarceration, and glared at them defiantly but remained silent.

The miller looked embarrassed by the whole situation and, face flushing red, turned away from his fellow villager and went back to his work.

John pulled a short, slim length of rope from beneath his cloak and used it to bind their prisoner's hands behind his back.

"Let's go," Robin shouted over the near-deafening squeak and rumbling of the mill's mechanisms.

"And," John added his own great booming voice to his captain's, "don't even think about trying to escape you raping scum, or you'll feel my quarterstaff on the back of your skull."

"Better tell Broadhurst you're off," the miller said, following them as they left the building and emerged into the street again. "That's his house over there."

"Bollocks," John grumbled, realising the headman's house was in the opposite direction to the inn, and their horses.

"At least the sun's up," Robin smiled, pushing their prisoner ahead of them. "Should be a nicer day than yesterday, so we'll make good time and be back in Nottingham before we know it."

* * *

The headman's house was much bigger than most of the other houses in the village. It sat slightly apart from the rest boasting two storeys and glazed windows rather than just wooden shutters.

Only one other house they passed came close to it in size, but that appeared deserted, despite being in a good state of repair.

The door opened before Robin had a chance to knock, and William Broadhurst greeted them with a smile.

"God give you good day," the headman said, gesturing them inside, but Robin rejected the invitation with a wave of his hand.

"We have no time to waste, we must return to the sheriff as soon as possible, before the weather turns again. We just wanted you to know we'd taken charge of the prisoner."

"I'm relieved to hear it. Be wary of him," Broadhurst warned, throwing Tanner a nervous glance. "He can be violent when angry. As his poor victim will attest."

Robin glanced at their captive but the man remained silent.

"Don't worry about us," Little John rumbled, his eyes fixed on Tanner. "If it comes to violence there's none better than me and Robin."

A pretty young woman appeared in the doorway, her blue eyes wide as she looked from William the headman to the sullen prisoner.

Then with a cry of "You lying bitch!"Tanner suddenly threw himself forward toward the girl, his face twisted in a murderous rage, but he slipped in the snow, hindered by his bindings.

As Tanner crashed to the ground face-first, the headman and the startled girl jerked backwards in fright. In contrast, Little John bent down and slapped Tanner hard across the side of the head.

It was enough. The fight left the prisoner and he simply lay in the snow, eyes pressed tightly shut against the obvious agony the giant's blow had caused.

"You're his victim?" Robin asked, eyeing the girl who looked as if she wanted the ground to swallow her whole.

"She is," William Broadhurst replied. "As you can see from her injuries. Show them, Joan." He gestured to the nervous woman.

Joan stared at the fallen captive for a few moments before reaching up and drawing the collar of her tunic down to reveal her pale neck. Pale, that was, apart from the purple and yellow bruises which had clearly been made by grasping, forceful fingers.

"He did that, lady?" Robin demanded, glaring down at Tanner who had pushed himself to his knees in the snow watching the girl venomously.

"He did," she whispered, her eyes flicking from the prisoner to the headman.

"As I say," Broadhurst repeated, "he is a very violent man. Please be careful. Never take your eyes from him!"

"God curse you both," Tanner cried, but he made no more threatening movements. John's blow had cautioned him well enough against further attempts at violence towards Joan or the headman.

"Come on," Robin said to his lieutenant brusquely. "Let's get this son of a whore to Nottingham." He nodded farewell to Broadhurst, then looked at Joan with a reassuring smile. "Don't worry yourself about this man any more. We'll make sure justice is served."

The grim-faced lawmen walked back towards the alehouse, shoving Luke Tanner ahead of them, the memory of the bruises on the young woman's neck playing on both their minds.

* * *

As Robin had foreseen, the previous day's snow held off, and a bright sun occasionally peeped out from between the clouds as the party of three rode back towards Nottingham. It was still cold, despite the sunshine, so the ground remained hard with frost rather than turning to slush.

"We should have this one in the sheriff's cells soon enough," John said, cheerfully. "Then justice will be served."

The prisoner tried to spit into the road in disgust but his lips were numb from the frost and the speckles of saliva dribbled down his chin. His hands were bound before him so he could grasp the horse's bridle, but even so, he made no effort to wipe the spittle.

He looked close to tears, in fact.

Neither Robin nor John said much for the rest of the morning while Tanner remained completely silent, and the miles passed under their mounts' hooves until, a short while before midday, Robin called a halt. They hadn't set a hard pace, but the horses' sides were steaming and it seemed a good time to rest and have some refreshments.

John moved to help their captive down from the saddle while Robin led the horses to a brook which ran parallel to the road, allowing them to drink their fill before tethering them to some elm trees.

"Ow, watch what you're doing you damn oaf," Tanner cried, as John inadvertently twisted his arm while helping him down to the ground.

Before Hood could intervene, Little John, face twisted in anger, grabbed hold of the prisoner by the neck, lifted him clear off the grass, and threw him as if he were just a child.

"Don't you talk to me like that, you piece of filth. You're lucky you're still alive – if it were up to me we'd just throw a rope over that branch there–" he pointed to a thick bough in the nearest elm "–and watch you swing from it for what you did that poor girl."

Tanner writhed on the hard, frosty grass, teeth clenched at the pain in his back and shoulders but before the situation could deteriorate any further Robin strode across and laid a hand on his friend's arm.

"Enough. It's not our job to judge him. We're just supposed to take him to the sheriff in one piece." He gestured to the horses and smiled to offset his hard tone. "Find us some meat and ale, will you. That inn-keep's pack should be well stocked for a fine meal."

Mollified somewhat, the giant moved to do as he was ordered while Robin bent to drag the downed captive up into a sitting position.

"We'll share the provisions with you but from now on I'd advise you not to antagonise us or things will go badly for you."

* * *

The rest of the day passed without incident although it started to rain, turning the road into a slippery, slushy mess that slowed their passage markedly.

The prisoner had held a sullen silence ever since the argument with John, and Robin, watching the water stream down the man's face expected no further trouble. John was a genial character most of the time, but when he threatened someone with violence it usually made them back down.

"I think we'll stop here and set up camp," the bailiff said, spotting a couple of holly trees which would afford them some shelter and allow a campfire which they could use to warm their food. "That rain's made the footing treacherous and we'll not find a better place to spend the night."

The rich green leaves and red berries of the tree contrasted against the gloominess of the road and seemed somehow cheering as John gladly set to work starting a small fire. Robin helped Tanner down from the saddle this time, and the man came as meekly as a lamb.

"I'll go and find some more kindling," the lawman said to Little John. "I think the inn-keep said he'd packed some sausages in there, didn't he? They'd go down nicely with some warm bread and ale."

John nodded agreement, a great smile appearing from within his beard, and turned to search through the saddlebags for the food as Robin, with a last glance at their captive, disappeared into the rain to find enough fuel to last the night.

Luke Tanner watched Hood go and then turned to the giant who was happily whistling a tune as he brought the provisions out by the little fire. Both lawmen were ignorant to the fact their prisoner wasn't as tightly bound as he appeared.

When he'd been incarcerated in the bowels of the water mill he'd noticed various supplies stored there. The usual things you'd expect in a cellar, like salt, spices and casks of ale, but, most interestingly to him – oil.

Tanner wasn't sure if it was intended for cooking or perhaps to lubricate the workings of the mill, but before he'd been taken by Hood and his lieutenant, he'd smeared the stuff on his wrists and the rope that held them. Not enough that anyone would notice, but sufficient to make them a little more pliable.

Now, as Robin became lost amongst the trees, the prisoner – who'd been clenching and unclenching his fists for hours now, working the bindings ever looser – desperately dragged his left hand free of its hemp manacle. He stared, wide-eyed, at Little John, praying to God the man wouldn't turn around, as he furiously squeezed his right hand free too, and then slowly got to his feet.

Attacking the giant seemed futile. Luke wasn't a fighter and he knew, even with the element of surprise, he'd never be able to defeat the legendary lawman.

Instead, he lifted a burning twig from the campfire, crept up behind John who was rooting in his pack for a pot to cook their dinner in, and held the small flame against the man's cloak.

"Please God, come on," the prisoner prayed desperately, as the sodden material steamed but failed to ignite. If this didn't work he'd never get another chance, for they'd beat him senseless and tie his bonds tighter than ever.

"Please, God!"

At last, John's cloak began to burn and Luke, breathing a silent prayer of thanks, stepped back, watching as the fire spread.

When the giant turned, wondering why the back of his legs felt so warm, he spotted Tanner, watching fearfully but, before he could attack, glanced down and realised the danger he was in.

"You little bastard. You set fire to me!"

John slapped ineffectually at the flaming garment, roaring in fear, and Tanner took his chance, sprinting off into the trees in the opposite direction Robin Hood had taken.

He was free!

* * *

"What the hell's going on?" Robin shouted, dashing back to the camp, where he saw John flapping his hands and dancing on the spot as flames licked around the bottom of his cloak. If their prisoner had still been safely tied up it would have been hugely comical.

But Luke Tanner was nowhere to be seen and, as warm as John might be, a chill ran down Robin's back.

"Oh for God's sake, roll in the slush," the bailiff ordered irritably, grabbing his big friend by the arm and hauling him down to the ground. The combination of water and their patting hands was enough to quickly extinguish the blaze and John sighed in relief.

"Where's Tanner?"

They stood up and peered into the gloom.

"He went in that direction," John deduced, spotting footprints in the soft ground. "Little devil sneaked up behind me and set alight to my clothes. Come on." He grabbed his quarterstaff – a massive length of oak which would be utterly lethal in his expert hands – and ran in the direction of the tracks, Robin hurrying along behind.

Tanner had a fair head start on them but his trail was easy enough to follow until they came to a point where the trees grew thickly and there was a choice of directions the fugitive might have taken. The branches might have lost their summer foliage but the ground there was harder and there were no obvious signs of footprints.

"We don't have time to waste searching for his trail," Robin decided. "The longer he's out of our hands the harder it'll be to find him. You go to the right and I'll go along here. Be careful," he warned. "If he's desperate enough to try and burn you alive, there's no telling what else he's capable of. We should have listened closer to Broadhurst's warnings about him."

John nodded and ran off through the trees, eyes scanning the area. "I hope he *does* attack me again – this time I won't be so gentle."

Robin couldn't blame his enraged lieutenant for his murderous mood, he just had to hope he came across their escapee before John did.

He drew his sword, trying to see any signs of Tanner's passage while also keeping a wary eye out for an ambush. Robin was a skilled swordsman with years of training and experience, and he had faster reflexes than most.

It was just as well, for he saw the branch whipping towards him an instant before it would have smashed into his face and he was able – just! – to dodge out of the way in time.

The stick flew past, completely missing its target, but he was thrown off balance and his legs slid out from under him, toppling him onto his side.

It gave Tanner another chance, and this time he made no mistake, smashing the branch down viciously on Robin's head.

Tanner's satisfied expression turned quickly to dismay though, as his weapon, sturdy as it had seemed, fell to pieces in his hand, so rotten was it from the damp weather.

Undoubtedly, the state of the wood saved Robin from being knocked out cold or worse, but he was still stunned by the blow, and the fugitive jumped onto his back, putting his right arm around the lawman's throat and squeezing for all he was worth.

"I'm sorry, bailiff, I truly am," the attacker sobbed, his voice almost hysterical. "I didn't want to hurt you but I won't let you arrest me for a crime I didn't commit."

Robin gagged, scrabbling to break Tanner's choke-hold but the smaller man was stronger than he looked, and fought with the desperation of one condemned. The lawman felt himself growing weaker with every heartbeat. He tried to shout for help, hoping John was somewhere close, but only a pitiful croak came out.

"I'm so sorry –" Tanner repeated, shifting his legs to gain even more leverage but momentarily loosening his hold on Robin.

It was just enough.

The bailiff threw his right fist up, hammering the knuckles into flesh and bone with every ounce of strength he could muster, and Tanner's grip fell away completely. Robin dropped down flat onto the wet grass, swinging a leg around and tripping his opponent who collapsed in an undignified heap.

Before the stunned man could renew his attack, Robin was up on his knees and had placed the point of his retrieved sword against Tanner's groin, pressing the tip in menacingly.

"One more move," he wheezed, "and I'll castrate you."

They remained there in the mud for a while, Robin sucking in great breaths of air and trying to clear his head, while Tanner gazed back at him from tear-filled, defeated eyes.

At last, the bailiff felt strong enough to stand and ordered his captive to do the same before prodding him with the sword into a slow, exhausted walk back to the camp.

* * *

Despite his aching head and John's singed pride their supper was a hearty and enjoyable one, and they were relieved to huddle around the campfire, prisoner in tow once again. It would have been rather embarrassing to return to Sir Henry in Nottingham without their charge, bruised and singed as they were.

When Robin returned to their base he'd found John already there. The giant had swiftly realised, from the lack of any tracks whatsoever, that he was on the wrong path and so returned to make sure no one made off with their horses and provisions.

He smiled grimly when his captain reappeared and strode across to give Tanner a couple of hard slaps for the trouble he'd caused, but Robin wearily waved him away and bade him prepare their meal.

After a couple of ales and a copious quantity of salted beef which was eaten in silence, the bailiff turned to the captive and eyed him curiously.

"Why did you say you didn't commit the crime you've been accused of? We heard the testimony from your headman and also your victim. It seems fairly straightforward to me."

Tanner stared back, chewing some of the bread he'd been given although he didn't have much of an appetite.

"What do you care?" he muttered, looking away into the dark shapes of the trees that surrounded the camp. "Just leave me alone. I won't be any more trouble to you. I know when I'm beat."

"You'd better not be any more trouble," John said. "Because I've had it now. Give me one more excuse and I'll break your fuc-"

"We've got all night to sit here in each other's company," Robin broke in, cutting off his friend's threat. "We might as well hear what you have to say. Why wouldn't you want to share it anyway, if you're as innocent as you claim?"

"What good would it do me?" Tanner asked plaintively. "The headman is the sheriff's cousin. Whose word will de Faucumberg believe? Besides, I heard all about you two – Broadhurst told me. You're just the sheriff's lapdogs, who do what they're told and kill anyone that gets in the way."

"The headman said that did he?" John demanded, eyebrows lowered indignantly. "I'll break his legs an' all if I see him again, the cheeky bastard."

"We haven't killed you though, have we?" Robin asked the prisoner. "Despite your violent escape attempt. I'd say that makes Broadhurst's description of us a little exaggerated, wouldn't you? So, I'll ask you again: what's your story? If you didn't rape that woman, why were you arrested for the crime?"

The rain had turned to snow again, and the prisoner huddled into his cloak, as close to the fire as he could manage, and stared at his guards in turn.

What harm could it do to share his side of the tale?

"Alright then," he muttered at last. "I'll tell you."

* * *

"Ah, Hood. You're finally back." Sir Henry de Faucumberg, High Sheriff of Nottingham and Yorkshire, smiled as his bailiff walked into the great hall in Nottingham Castle, but his eyebrows were lowered slightly in puzzlement. "Where the hell have you been? I expected you back here with that rapist a couple of days ago."

Robin shook his head at the cup of wine the sheriff offered him. "Aye, well, we had a bit of trouble on the road, my lord."

"So I see." The nobleman indicated the bruising around Robin's throat where Tanner had tried to choke him. "You brought the prisoner though, I assume? Good, bring him in then. I must make a record of the charges before we see what's to be done."

A scribe sat beside the sheriff's raised dais, ready, as ever, to record proceedings, while a number of blue-liveried soldiers stood guard at the sides of the high-ceilinged room. Robin and Little John had arrived in the afternoon, when most of the day's business had been done, so there were no petitioners or other members of the public in the hall as the bailiff strode to the great double doors and gestured to his lieutenant who stood in the corridor outside.

"Bring him, John."

The prisoner walked in, striding ahead of his massive jailer, head held high despite the bindings on his wrists and purple bruising around his eye and jaw.

"My Lord Sheriff," Robin announced, loudly, watching his superior closely. "Our prisoner from–"

"My cousin!" De Faucumberg jumped up from his high-backed chair and stared in amazement at, first, William Broadhurst, headman of Stapleford, to Robin, and then back again to the sullen captive. "What's the meaning of this, Hood? You were supposed to be bringing back some lowborn rapist, not a member of my own family."

"These men of yours are quite insane, Henry," Broadhurst blurted angrily. "They beat me and tied me up then forced me—" He tried to run towards the sheriff but John dragged him back by the collar, making the unfortunate man fall backwards onto the floor.

The guards moved forward, not sure what they should do in such a confused situation, but feeling like they had to at least show they were ready for action. They ignored, however, the fallen headman's command that they arrest Hood and Little John.

"I better explain," Robin said, and the sheriff, eyes blazing, nodded in agreement.

* * *

As they'd eaten their dinner by the campfire three nights earlier, Luke Tanner told them his whole story. And what a tale it was.

Luke's land butted William Broadhurst's and, for years, Broadhurst, a hugely wealthy man, had been trying to buy it from him. Tanner had no intention of ever selling up, though. The land, with his simple house, had been left to him by his father, who won favour with the young Earl of Lancaster during a campaign against the Scots in 1298.

The old soldier had saved the earl's life, almost decapitating a crazed invader just as he'd been about to plunge a sword into the nobleman's back.

The earl, when he'd grown in wealth and power a few years later, rewarded the soldier with the small parcel of land in Stapleford along with a modest stipend which was to be paid to him and his descendants for as long as their line continued.

This meant Luke Tanner never really had to work a day in his life once his father died and he took possession of the house and grounds. And, since he'd never properly learned the family trade, being no more a tanner than a surgeon, there was no good reason for the young man to sell his property to the headman as it would leave him without any income.

Eventually, William Broadhurst had grown irritated by the refusal of the man he regarded as lowborn scum to do as he was told, and took matters into his own hands.

"He must have paid Joan to say I raped her. I was asleep in my bed just the other night when a dozen men came for me, straight from the tavern by the smell of their breath. Didn't give me any chance to say my piece, just roughed me up and threw me down into the cellar of the mill, where you found me."

"I don't follow," Little John said, furrowing his brow. "How does setting you up as a criminal help Broadhurst get your land?"

"With me out of the way, all he has to do is extend his own fence around my property and, after a period of time it would become legally his. It's called 'adverse possession' and so-called 'noblemen' abuse it all the time."

"That's ridiculous," John hooted, clearly not believing a word. "The law wouldn't allow that."

"Aye, it would," Robin growled. "The rich and powerful can get away with anything. Look what happened to you when you couldn't afford to bribe the bailiff in your own village, John. You had to become an outlaw, didn't you? Your whole life ruined because you saved a little girl from a monster and the law twisted it to make you the criminal."[1]

The giant's smile faded to a confused, angry scowl as he recalled those terrible events years earlier [See *The Wolf and the Raven*].

"If anyone knows the law can be bent and abused by wealthy men, it's us," Robin went on. "I can't just take your word for all this though, Tanner. Do you have any proof? The sheriff's going to need some evidence."

Tanner looked downcast.

"No, I don't. Only my word. Unless you can somehow force a confession from Joan. She knows I didn't rape her."

"What about the bruises on her?" John demanded. "She didn't do that to herself."

They sat, staring into the flames for a long time, wondering what they could do to prove Tanner's innocence – or guilt – until, at last, Robin shrugged.

"I'm going to get some sleep. In the morning we'll go back to Stapleford and see what we find."

* * *

When they reached the village again the following day they rode straight to the inn where they bound Tanner and had the landlord lock him in one of the store rooms.

"Sorry, Luke," Robin said as they left him behind with just a candle for company. "But we still don't know whether your story is true or not. Until we do,

44

you'll remain under lock and key." He turned to the inn-keep and handed him a coin for his trouble. "We shouldn't be too long hopefully. I don't suppose you know anything about your headman trying to buy Tanner's land?"

"Not really," the man shrugged as they walked back to the front door. "I mean, aye, I've heard talk of it, it's not a secret. Why?"

"Never mind. Don't let the prisoner out of that room for any reason, all right? And trust me, he's a cunning devil so just leave him to himself."

They walked along the street towards William Broadhurst's house, through the snow which the villagers had already turned to dirty slush again with the passage of their feet and wagonwheels. People eyed them curiously as they went, wondering what their business might be.

"Why aren't we questioning any of these folk?" John wondered. "Wouldn't that be a good place to start?"

Robin shook his head. "Nah, you already saw the inn-keeper's reaction to our question about Broadhurst. People will be wary about talking to strangers, especially if we're asking about their powerful, wealthy headman."

"What are we going to do then?"

"I'm not sure," Robin admitted. "To be honest, there's not a lot we *can* do. We don't have the sheriff's authority to conduct an investigation. So... I'm just hoping God grants us some luck."

They reached the headman's property and Robin turned to John with a grin, then he looked up at the sky and mouthed a silent, "thank you".

"Looks like we've been lucky right enough," John nodded happily, eyeing the land about fifty yards away. "I'm guessing that's our prisoner's land those men are building a fence on."

Robin grunted and headed straight for the headman's door, pushing it open without knocking and striding inside, eyes scanning the gloomy interior.

A sound came to them from a room in the floor above and John placed a finger against his lips, leading the way up the steps as quietly as possibly.

The noises were unmistakeable and Robin wondered whether they should sneak back downstairs until the lovers were finished. He had no desire to embarrass the headman's wife since, as far as they knew, she was blameless in this whole sordid affair.

And then the woman spoke, and the eavesdroppers glanced at one another for a moment, before they moved forward decisively and burst into the bedchamber.

Joan – Luke Tanner's supposed victim – lay beneath the headman, her face a mask of anguish. Clearly she wasn't enjoying things as much as Broadhurst was.

As Robin and John watched, the headman arched his back and grasped the girl by the neck, squeezing hard, but his sadistic pleasure was cut short when he noticed her bulging eyes watching someone behind him.

He turned his head and saw the two huge lawmen, staring at him with undisguised loathing.

"What the hell are you doing in my house, you peasant scum?" He freed himself from the bedclothes, jumped onto the floor and charged at Robin, completely naked.

It was the first time the bailiff had ever been attacked by a nude man in a state of arousal and he was too shocked to respond until Broadhurst's fist hit him a glancing blow and he retaliated instinctively.

The headman screamed in agony and crumpled as Robin brought his knee up, ramming it between the naked assailant's legs. That was followed by a couple of devastating punches to the face which knocked Broadhurst senseless and Robin shook his head, stunned at the surreal, mercifully short fight.

John couldn't help laughing at his captain's dazed expression but Joan began to sob, instantly robbing the scene of its dark humour.

"I think it's pretty obvious what's been going on here," Robin spat. "Tanner was telling the truth after all. Come on you," he kicked the fallen, disgraced headman. "Get your damn clothes on, now, or we'll drag you into the street bollock naked so everyone in the village can see you. Move it!"

"Better wrap up warm too," John added grimly. "You've got a long journey ahead of you and it's a cold road to Nottingham."

* * *

Sir Henry de Faucumberg sat listening to Robin's tale, engrossed, the cup of wine in his hand all but forgotten.

"You have the other man – the falsely accused rapist – here with you? We can add his testimony to the record? Yes? Good, bring him in then. What about the woman – Joan was it?"

Robin shook his head as a guard opened the door and Luke Tanner was ushered in. "No, my lord, she was in a terrible state, I didn't think it wise to force her to make the journey here. As long as she knows there's no danger from him, though–" he jerked his head towards Broadhurst "–she promised to give a full account to the local bailiff."

The sheriff leaned back, remembering the cup in his hand and draining it before placing it on his long table.

"What do you have to say for yourself, cousin?" he demanded. "Can you deny any of Hood's story? Ah, never mind, I don't want to hear it. Take him to the dungeon."

Two of the guards came forward but Broadhurst swung his bound wrists, clumsily striking the nearest with his fists, then ran for the door.

"Stop him!"

The cry hadn't even burst from de Faucumberg's mouth before Little John had spun his quarterstaff and slammed it into the panicked fugitive's ribs. The man flew sideways, clattering into the wall, then collapsed into a crying, mewling heap. The guards had no sympathy for him though and he was dragged from the room, mumbling pleas for mercy.

The room was silent at last and the sheriff rubbed tiredly at his bearded face.

"What'll happen to him?"

De Faucumberg waved a hand dismissively at Robin's question.

"His crimes – larceny and possibly rape as well – are serious but I doubt he'll hang for them. Abjuration or, more likely, a fine will be his punishment. He'll have to pay the lady a sizeable sum for his treatment of her, and–"

"A fine," Tanner burst out, so angry that he forgot where he was. "After all he's done? All the trouble he's caused?"

"Doesn't seem right." Little John rumbled in agreement. "A fine means nothing to a man as wealthy as that, Sir Henry."

"That all depends on the size of the fine," de Faucumberg replied in a hard voice before he turned his gaze on the wronged villager. "It will probably be quite a while before the Justice in Eyre will be around to hear his case. In the meantime, while he rots in the dungeon someone might erect a fence on his land and incorporate it into their own holdings, rather as he planned to do to you. If you get my meaning."

Tanner stared for a moment before the sheriff's words sank in, then his eyes widened and a grin slowly spread across his face.

"That law you mentioned – 'adverse possession'? Well, it's not really a law but if you return here in a few weeks with the deeds to your property I'll make sure they're all legal, including any extra land you might accrue in that time..."

He stood up and stretched, rolling his head and groaning with exhaustion before looking down at Robin and John. "It's about time I retired for the day. Well done on the success of your mission you two, you can expect a bonus in your wages."

"Thank you, my lord," Luke Tanner cried, eyes filling with tears, as Robin ushered him from the hall. "Thank you. I never thought it possible, but justice has truly been served this day."

"Come on," Robin said as they left the stone corridors behind and stepped out into the courtyard. "You can buy us a drink or two."

"Aye, let's find an alehouse," John agreed with a grin. "Plenty of them about. But first, let's find a tailor." He grasped Tanner by the shoulder and glared balefully down at him, eyes twinkling mischievously. "You owe me a new cloak."

THE END

Author's Note

I was surprised to find I'd never written an author's note for the original Kindle version of this story so here is an exclusive for paperback readers!

The Prisoner was written mostly in my car, on a tiny laptop, during breaks at my day-job. As you probably already know if you've read *Friar Tuck and the Christmas Devil*, I really love winter, and *The Prisoner*, with its snowy setting, allowed me to explore that season again. The original title was going to be *The Stapleford Prisoner* but when Amazon offered to make the novelette part of their select Kindle Singles Program we decided that title was a bit too long and went with the snappier *The Prisoner* which also looked better on their fantastic wintry cover art.

(Incidentally, I don't own that cover art or the art for "The Escape", which is why it doesn't appear anywhere in this book. Check them out on the Kindle versions, they look really nice).

The legal aspects of the story might be somewhat exaggerated but the idea of a rich man trying to become even richer at a poor man's expense fitted very well with the whole Robin Hood mythos. I hope you enjoyed the "baddie" getting his comeuppance. This is one of my favourite stories in the whole series.

Steven A. McKay
October 27th, 2017

THE

RESCUE

Wakefield, England 1325AD
Summer

It was mid-morning and a little chilly although the sun was threatening to come out and Matilda Hood sat bundled in a heavy cloak as she worked with a basket of goose feathers, fletching arrow shafts for her father. She watched contentedly as her infant son, Arthur, played with some of the other village children, her fingers moving nimbly, expertly, despite the cold.

She hoped to finish as many arrows as possible before midday when she would head home and heat some pottage for their midday meal. It was just her and Arthur today, since Robin, her husband, was away in one of the neighbouring towns on a job for the sheriff, Sir Henry de Faucumberg. He wasn't expected back for another couple of days, so she'd come to help her father with his work.

Henry Fletcher was inside, cutting the wood that would become his arrows and grumbling about the unseasonable cold. He'd been happy to see his daughter and grandson that morning though since he had a lot of work to get through and, as a result, appreciated Matilda's help and, of course, her company.

The Fletchers were a close family and Robin had been accepted readily into the fold, as had his younger, sixteen-year-old sister Marjorie, who appeared now, hurrying up the path towards Matilda.

"Have you seen Sam?" she demanded, her eyes darting about the garden anxiously. "I've not seen him since I let him out for a piss this morning. It's not like him to run off."

Matilda shook her head but smiled reassuringly. Marjorie had been given a puppy a few months ago when a local bitch gave birth to a litter and the girl had grown close to the animal which she'd named Sam. It followed her everywhere although, being a mastiff, it had grown much bigger than the excitable furry baby it had once been. It was a placid beast and Matilda had been happy enough to let Arthur ride on its back at times.

"Maybe there's a bitch in season," Matilda smiled, trying to calm her sister-in-law's fears. "I'm sure he'll be back soon enough."

Marjorie didn't reply. Her eyes hadn't stopped scanning the village and now she hurried off in the direction of the Calder.

"I'm heading home to make some food for Arthur and me in a little while," Matilda shouted at her back. "Come and join us if you like."

"Can't," Marjorie shouted over her shoulder. "I'm heading down to the river to see if Sam's there. He loves swimming but there was that heavy rain yesterday..." She trailed off as she disappeared into the trees, the fear of her dog drowning evident in her voice.

Matilda watched her go, fingers never stopping as she fletched the arrow shafts with practised ease. A short time later, around midday, she called on Arthur, waved goodbye to her father inside the workshop and then walked the short distance back to their home for something to eat and drink.

* * *

"Have you seen—"

Matilda broke in before her mother-in-law could finish her sentence. "No, I've not seen the dog. Still missing then?"

Martha Hood shook her head, eyes wide. "I'm not bothered about the dog," she said. "It's Marjorie I'm looking for."

Matilda had spent the last hour at home, first sharing a meal with Arthur and then mending some of the lad's clothes which were forever getting torn. She met Martha's gaze now, only mildly concerned. Matilda had trained the girl to fight and knew she could take care of herself well enough.

"She went down to the river looking for that dog earlier. Has she not come back yet?"

"No." The older woman wrung her hands and little Arthur wandered across, raising his arms to her with a grin. She peered down distractedly before finally lifting him and cuddling him in tight. "I don't know where she is. This isn't like her at all, Matilda. I'm worried, especially now you say she went to the river. There was that heavy rain..."

"All right. You take Arthur to your house," Matilda leaned in to kiss her son on the forehead, "and I'll go and find her."

Martha nodded, her expression grateful. "My husband, John, is out looking for her too. Maybe he's already found her. I'll take this little angel back to mine and we'll see, shall we? Shall we?" She tweaked Arthur's nose and he squealed in delight, burying his face in her shoulder before pulling back so she could do it again.

"Off you go, then," Matilda said, waving. "Don't worry though – I'll find her soon enough."

She watched them leave then ran to the bed chamber and pulled her sword in its leather sheath from the wardrobe, tying it around her slim waist and grabbing her longbow. As she did so, another sleek black weapon caught her eye and she lifted that too before hurrying out into the afternoon sunshine.

* * *

When Marjorie had pushed through the foliage towards the Calder she'd feared only one thing: that her dog Sam had fallen or jumped into the water and been carried away to his death. The hound was a fine swimmer but she knew the swollen river could kill man or beast within minutes if they became trapped in the reeds or pulled under by the current, no matter how strong they were.

When she reached the water her heart had leapt as the muddy grass showed the sign of paw-prints, and they were big enough that she knew they were probably her pet's.

As she followed them a thrill of fear ran down her back and she bent to examine a number of other prints that seemed to merge with Sam's.

Around half a dozen men, accompanied by as many dogs, had passed this way not long ago and Sam had joined or been taken by them. That was bad enough, but her eyes settled on heavy ruts in the grass and, when she realised what they might mean her blood ran cold and she broke into a run.

Sam had been taken by bear-baiters.

* * *

Matilda came upon the same tracks a while later and instantly knew what they meant. She saw the smaller prints left by her sister-in-law and she followed them at speed along the river bank, hoping desperately that she'd be in time.

Marjorie Hood wasn't physically imposing like her famous brother Robin – she'd been a sickly child who'd only recently grown in strength and confidence when she'd learned to fight under Matilda's tutelage. But she was no match for the party they were trailing now.

The sun had risen high in the sky and reflected blindingly off the fast-flowing waters of the River Calder on the right side of the road.

"No!" Matilda pulled up, eyes wide in shock and fear as she spotted the slim figure lying prone on the thick green grass ahead. "Oh, please no," she gasped, hurrying forward and pressing a hand to Marjorie's cheek.

It was warm. Thank God!

There was a bruise on the girl's forehead though and, as Matilda knelt by her, Marjorie opened her eyes, rolled onto her side and retched on the ground, her body shuddering pitifully as only yellow bile came out.

"Are you all right? What the hell happened? How could you be so stupid to follow those men? Men like that are used to danger, you're no match for-"

"They have Sam," Marjorie broke in breathlessly, still trying to spit the stringy remnants of bile from her lips. "I have to get him back."

Matilda grabbed the girl by the arm as she tried to rise, holding her down. "You can't. They'll kill you. They did that to your head?"

Marjorie reached up and gingerly felt the large bruise, wincing slightly as she felt the size of it. "Aye. I tried to talk to them but they were having none of it. They were going to throw me in the river but I told them Robin Hood was my brother and they must have decided not to kill me after all. I almost wish they had."

She bent down and retched again but it passed soon enough and she sucked in a great lungful of air, her eyes settling on the weapon in Matilda's left hand.

"My crossbow." She reached out and took it from her friend with a grim nod. "This will even things up a little. Thank you for bringing it."

"You left it at mine the last time we practised. Thought it might come in handy. But-" she shook her head firmly "- you're not going after those men. Your life is worth more than a dog's. Come on. We can tell Robin about it when he gets home; maybe he'll be able to find them and return Sam to you."

"Sam will be dead by then! I heard them saying they were going to Normanton for a show."

"Sam is a big, powerful dog," Matilda argued. "It would take a lot to kill him."

Marjorie turned and started walking, fast. "He's soft, despite his size. I can't bear the thought of him fighting that.... A bear for God's sake!" She gasped in anguish then set her jaw. "I'm going after the bastards."

Matilda watched her sister-in-law's retreating back then, knowing it was useless and feeling angry herself at the situation, jogged after her, checking her sword

was loose in its scabbard and her bowstring safely in
its pouch.

* * *

The dog thieves weren't travelling very fast since
their show in Normanton wasn't until the following
afternoon and the ox pulling their heavy cart with the
bear in it was slow, so the two young women
managed to catch up to them when they were still
about a mile from their destination. They'd stopped to
rest and lounged on the grass or on fallen trees,
drinking ale and talking in rough, hard voices to one
another.

"There they are," Matilda said, flattening herself
against the trunk of a thick oak and watching the
party ahead. Six big men with leashed dogs of various
breeds and sizes, and one enormous brown bear,
locked in a cage that sat atop the ox-drawn cart.
"What are we going to do now?"

Marjorie crouched down behind a juniper bush and
stared in silence along the narrow road. Clearly,
trying to reason with the men was useless. Her
battered skull was proof of that.

She loaded a quarrel into her black crossbow – an
exquisite, masterful little weapon which had once
belonged to The Raven, Sir Guy of Gisbourne – and
smiled. It was supposed to be a confident, wolfish
grin like her brother sometimes did, but her fear was
obvious.

"We can't just start killing them," Matilda growled,
realising they really hadn't thought this through.
"Stealing someone's dog doesn't warrant a death
sentence. We'll be hanged for it!"

Marjorie nodded but there was a twinkle in her eye now. She might not have Robin's massive physique, but she'd inherited some of his cunning.

"This is what we're going to do..."

* * *

"Hey, arsehole!"

The six men looked round as one at the voice, their faces angry but not fearful. They had their beasts and their weapons to defend themselves after all, but no-one likes being insulted.

Especially not by a skinny young girl.

"It's that little bitch from earlier," one of the men grunted, rolling his eyes irritably. "I told you we should have chucked her in the river."

"Aye," Marjorie shouted agreement. "You should have. I told you who my brother is, didn't I?"

The men knew very well who Robin Hood was. Everyone in the north of England had heard of the fabled wolf's head and his ruthless gang. Word was he'd been pardoned and now worked for the law but still, tales of his brutality were sung all across the country.

The pack of dogs had begun to sense the anxiety emanating from their masters and some of them began to whine or growl. Marjorie's heart leapt as she spotted Sam, tail between his legs as if he'd been beaten, and she gritted her teeth, bringing up the crossbow and pointing it at the nearest of the men.

"Your brother ain't here lass," the man spat, stepping towards her. "And this time you *are* going for a swim."

There was a snap and a shocking blur of motion as an arrow tore from the thick summer foliage behind the girl and hit the approaching man's thigh. The missile buried itself in the muscle so hard that it knocked him off his feet and he screamed in agony as the excited dogs began barking and straining at the ropes that tethered them to the cart. In contrast, the great brown bear in the cage looked on in silence.

"My brother *is* here, lad," Marjorie hissed, eyes moving from the fallen man to his stunned companions. "And so are his friends."

The men didn't seem to know what to do now. They were hard men but they'd never been in a situation like this before, where unseen assailants were able to pick them off at leisure. Four of them shrank back close to the cart, but one, braver than his brothers, drew a long knife from his belt and charged at Marjorie.

She stood her ground, knowing any show of fear would shatter the illusion she was trying to create, but the sight of the enraged man bearing down on her almost turned her knees to water.

His knife rose high in the air and he came so close that the blackheads on his nose seemed enormous to the girl but, just before he reached her another goose-feather shafted arrow broke through the lush foliage, this time from the other side, and hammered into the man.

Christ above, she's good, Marjorie thought in relief as her would-be assailant fell sideways, roaring with pain at the vicious iron broadhead buried deep in his shoulder. Feeling more sure of herself now she aimed her crossbow at the fallen man and stared at him with emotionless eyes.

"All I want is my dog back. You're not making him fight that brute for the pleasure of a few villagers in Normanton." She looked up at the man huddled nearest to Sam. "You! Cut him free now or another of you bastards will have a tale to tell your mates. Shot by Robin Hood! Only the next one might not be as lucky as your two downed friends – my brother's the best longbowman in all England but even he sometimes hits a target in the wrong place."

"You cowardly scum," one of the men roared to the forest in general. "Hiding in the trees rather than coming forward and fighting like a man."

"Shut up," his compatriot next to him shouted fearfully. "This is how they always worked in the stories. Ambushing people from the safety of the trees. But Hood can best any man with a blade if he feels like it. So shut yer hole and cut that little bastard's dog loose!"

The rest of the crouching men murmured agreement and so Sam's rope was slashed through and the big hound sprinted happily towards her, tongue lolling stupidly, slavers dripping from his great maw.

Matilda knew she couldn't lower her crossbow so she slowly backed away from the two prone men who remained where they were, murderous expressions on their faces at her retreat. Sam was by her side, making little jumps every so often in happiness at seeing his mistress.

"You'll be sorry for this," the one with the arrow in his thigh grunted, face pale as he grasped the injury. "You can't go around shooting people, even if we did take your damn dog."

"Which we didn't," one of the other men cried. "It followed us itself." He stepped forward as one of the furious yelping dogs lunged at him, straining at its leash, and yet another arrow erupted from the trees to thud into the lush grass just a yard in front of him.

"Enough," he screeched. "Take your damn mutt and go! We'll be reporting this to the bailiff once we reach Normanton though, you bet your life on that."

Marjorie shook her head angrily at the suggestion. "You report what you like. You whoresons stole my dog then beat me unconscious before trying to throw me to my death in the river. You're lucky—"

Her words were torn from her as Sam, stupid, friendly Sam the one hundred and eighty pound mastiff that wouldn't hurt a lamb, jumped up and licked her face, shoving her sideways. She was so shocked that her finger pressed the trigger of the crossbow, firing the bolt uselessly into the grass and she shouted at the dog to get off.

He did, but she panicked and her fingers fumbled with the mechanism as she tried to load another quarrel into it. The man with the arrow in his shoulder suddenly jumped to his feet, so furious at being bested by a girl that he ignored the longbowman hidden in the trees and threw himself on Marjorie, his good hand squeezing mercilessly around her throat.

* * *

There was no way Matilda could take the attacker down from her hiding place in the trees. If she tried to shoot him there was every chance she'd hit Marjorie instead.

63

Her mind whirled as she desperately tried to figure out how to save her friend. If she broke from her cover and used her sword to kill the man his companions would realise they'd been fooled and set the crazed dogs on them. Those animals weren't like big, friendly Sam – they were fighting dogs, experienced and scarred from numerous bloody, brutal battles with the bear and, probably, one another too.

She stared in anguish as the man throttled Marjorie who tried to fight back but, pinned beneath his much greater weight as she was, had no way of freeing herself. Sam simply stood watching in confusion, his tail wagging.

Matilda's inaction gave heart to the rest of the bear-baiters who, realising "Robin Hood" wasn't attacking any more, had begun to slowly move towards the ropes that tethered their dogs to the cart.

This had all been a huge mistake. They were going to die for the sake of a stupid dog.

* * *

Marjorie could feel herself losing consciousness as she tried in vain to throw the man off. He was much too heavy and the way he was lying on top of her meant she could get no leverage into her arms or legs for a punch or kick to his eyes or groin.

Fear brought tears to her eyes and she saw Sam, looking down at her, his massive head tilted to one side in puzzlement.

"Get him," she gasped, the words nothing more than a croak. "Get him!"

Her terror gave her strength and she somehow managed to squeeze enough air through her vocal chords to form the words at last, even if it was too late.

Instantly, the weight fell from her and she sucked in deep breaths, wondering what had happened. The screaming penetrated her oxygen-starved brain at last and she groggily turned her gaze to the left, where Sam was tearing her attacker's throat to bloody pieces with his sharp young teeth.

She lay for a time, staring up at the terrible scene, trying to regain her senses. Then the reality hit her and she knew she had to move now, before the remaining men let the dogs out and came for her and her hidden companion in the undergrowth.

And Sam.

She rolled onto her belly and pushed herself up onto one knee, shocked at the sight of her usually-equable dog, his muzzle coated in crimson gore, as he padded across to her and licked her cheek.

Too shocked to complain, Marjorie grasped the dog's back and used him to drag herself to her feet.

"Good boy. Good boy," she muttered over and over, her vision blurred by tears of fear and shock.

There was another snap from the longbow in the trees as she staggered away, Sam at her side, back along the road to Wakefield, the sounds of barking dogs and outraged, shouting men barely registering in her ears.

* * *

Before they returned home Matilda led Sam to the Calder and washed the bloody mess from his face.

The giant dog stood placidly while he was cleaned and the young woman could still hardly believe it had killed a man.

When they walked back into Wakefield word spread of their safe return but neither of them told the tale of where they'd been all day. Instead, they said the dog had gone after a bitch in heat in a neighbouring village and Marjorie had fallen chasing the beast, knocking herself out and bruising her head. Matilda had then, she said, found both dog and stunned girl and brought them home.

It was dark by this time and the vicious purple fingerprints on Marjorie's throat were hidden by the shadows.

She wore a high-necked cloak for days until they'd faded.

No lawmen ever came to question them over the death of the mauled man, and they never mentioned the incident to Robin, but a few days later word reached the village of a wonderful bear-baiting show that had taken place in Normanton before the troupe had moved on to the north with their beasts.

Sam lived to the ripe old age of sixteen but never killed again, instead spending much of his time chasing after his tail.

He never did manage to catch it.

THE END

Author's Note

The first story in this book, "The Escape", was originally given away for free to the few people who signed up to my email list. Then Amazon liked it and decided to sell it as part of their Kindle Singles Program which was fantastic for me but meant I had to write something new to give away to my email list subscribers.

The result was "The Rescue".

The dog was named after my own long-departed, much-loved, canine companion Sam, and the tale gave me the chance to let two of the Forest Lord's strong female characters show their mettle.

I don't have that many subscribers to my email list and it always seemed to me that "The Rescue" should be available to a wider audience, hence its inclusion here.

Steven A. McKay

October 27th 2017

Afterword

That's it – The End! Thank you so much for buying this omnibus edition of the short Forest Lord tales. I really hope you enjoyed them and will check out my other books if you haven't already. Tell your friends about them too, and look out for my new series, starring Bellicus the warrior-druid, coming soon.

Think of a combination of Robin, Little John and Friar Tuck and you'd be close to Bellicus – a giant of a man who fights like a demon but takes his spiritual responsibilities very seriously. He has been a fantastic character to create and I'm very hopeful fans of the Forest Lord stories will really like *The Druid.*

Cheers!

Steven A. McKay,

Old Kilpatrick, Scotland,

October 26th, 2017

P.S. Please don't forget to leave a review for this collection on Amazon and/or Goodreads!

Forest Lord Reading Order

This is how I suggest you read the series, but the year each story is set in is listed if you'd rather read chronologically:

Wolf's Head -1321

Knight of the Cross -1309

The Wolf and the Raven – 1322

"The Escape" – 1323 *

Rise of the Wolf – 1323

Friar Tuck and the Christmas Devil – 1323

"The Prisoner" – 1325 *

"The Rescue" – 1325 *

Blood of the Wolf – 1326

The Abbey of Death – 1328

Printed in Great Britain
by Amazon